THE GREAT
ALEXANDER
THE GREAT

Story and pictures by Joe Lasker

THE VIKING PRESS
NEW YORK

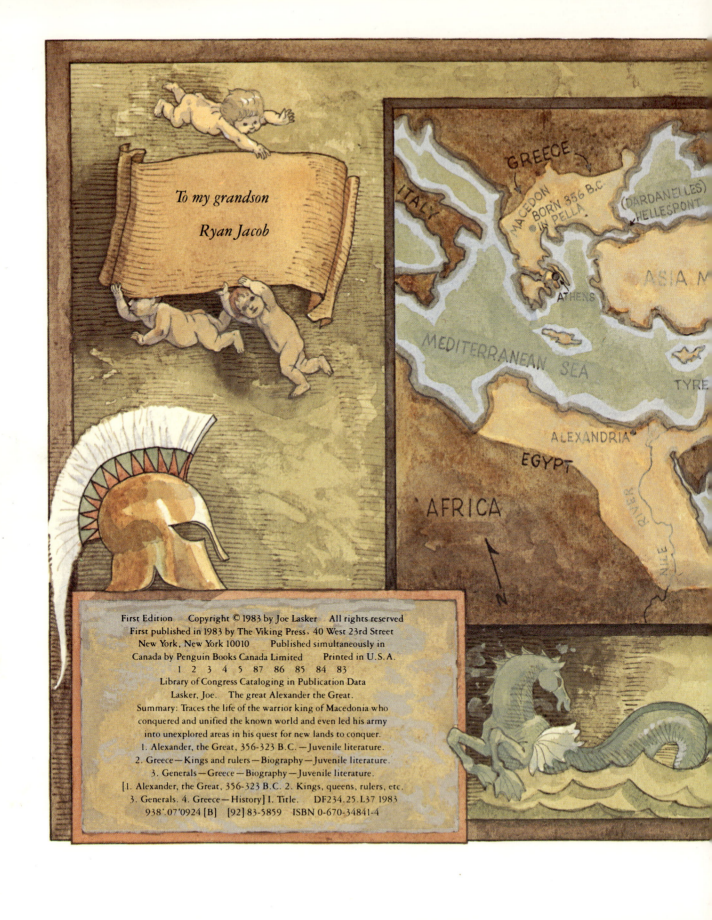

To my grandson

Ryan Jacob

First Edition   Copyright © 1983 by Joe Lasker   All rights reserved
First published in 1983 by The Viking Press, 40 West 23rd Street
New York, New York 10010   Published simultaneously in
Canada by Penguin Books Canada Limited   Printed in U.S.A.
1 2 3 4 5 87 86 85 84 83
Library of Congress Cataloging in Publication Data
Lasker, Joe.   The great Alexander the Great.
Summary: Traces the life of the warrior king of Macedonia who
conquered and unified the known world and even led his army
into unexplored areas in his quest for new lands to conquer.
1. Alexander, the Great, 356-323 B.C. — Juvenile literature.
2. Greece — Kings and rulers — Biography — Juvenile literature.
3. Generals — Greece — Biography — Juvenile literature.
[1. Alexander, the Great, 356-323 B.C. 2. Kings, queens, rulers, etc.
3. Generals. 4. Greece — History] I. Title.   DF234.25.L37 1983
938'.07'0924 [B]   [92] 83-5859   ISBN 0-670-34841-4

CHINA

CASPIAN SEA

BUCEPHALA

JHELUM R.

RIVER

INDUS

PERSIA
(IRAN)

DIES 323 B.C. IN
•BABYLON

RUSALEM

INDIA

ARABIA

PERSIAN GULF

0 100 200 300 400 MILES

ARABIAN SEA

ACK SEA

R.

ALEXANDER'S EMPIRE

The magnificent black stallion reared, throwing the king's stablemaster to the ground. His assistants shouted at the fiery horse, pulling roughly on the halter.

Philip, king of Macedonia, a region of northern Greece, stood looking on. His ministers and generals pressed about him, talking of war.

Close by stood Alexander, the king's seven-year-old son. "He's the most beautiful horse I've ever seen," said the prince. "But they are frightening him."

The shaken stablemaster limped over to the king. "Sire, I beg you not to buy this horse. He is unmanageable." Philip nodded in agreement.

Alexander pushed his way into the circle of men around the king. "No! Don't listen! He's a good horse!" he shouted at his father. The bearded elders were astonished at Alexander's rudeness. Philip, annoyed, glanced down at his son, then went on discussing war.

"Father! Listen!" demanded the boy. "They don't know how to handle him!"

The king's one good eye flashed in anger. "Are you telling me my horseman can't handle horses?"

"No, sir—well, I mean, I think I know how to control him." Everybody laughed at Alexander.

"And after you tame him, will you pay for him?" mocked the king.

Alexander would not back down. "I will somehow."

"All right, by Zeus," growled Philip. "I'll bet you the price of the horse you can't ride him."

Silent and anxious, everybody watched the young prince. Without hesitation he ran toward the horse. As he came closer, Alexander's run changed to a slow walk. The great black stallion loomed larger than when seen from a safe distance.

Alexander's heart pounded with fear, but he could not turn back now. He had been taught that courage and honor counted for more than life itself.

Slowly he reached for the reins. He could see that the animal was as frightened as he was. Pity mingled with Alexander's fear. Perhaps his feelings were sensed by the horse, for he allowed Alexander to turn him around, facing into the sun.

The boy lightly swung himself onto the horse's bare back. The stallion leaped forward, powerful hooves pounding the earth. Alexander bent low, talking softly into the horse's ear while applying just enough pressure to keep him headed into the sun. Gradually the horse grew calmer. Alexander straightened up, laughing joyously. The horse galloped free. Everybody cheered. Then Alexander cantered back to his father.

"Well done, my son!" Philip cried. "What magic did you use?"

"No magic, Father," Alexander answered. "He was frightened by his own shadow. I turned him to face into the sun. When he no longer saw his shadow, he was mine."

This horse and rider cast their shadow across the world. Bucephalus became the most famous horse in history. He never let anyone but Alexander ride him. When Alexander was preparing to mount, the noble horse would lower his body to help him on. In battle Alexander always rode Bucephalus.

When Philip died, Alexander was twenty. He became king of Macedonia, and war became his business. He won every battle, even when his army was heavily outnumbered. Just as he had understood Bucephalus, Alexander understood what his opponents were planning. Wearing a white plume on his helmet for the enemy to see, he won the devotion of his men by always leading them in battle.

"The gods watch over me for I am the son of Zeus," boasted Alexander.

At first Alexander waged war to unite the different regions of Greece. After two years he had unified all Greece. Then he marched on to do battle with the Persians, whose powerful empire lay only a mile offshore, across the Hellespont.

Alexander fought his way across Asia Minor and Arabia until he came to the city of Tyre, an island half a mile off the Mediterranean seacoast.

"Pass it by for now and push on," urged his generals. "Let us first defeat the Persians."

"We can't attack that fortified island. They have a navy—we don't."

"For a thousand years Tyre has withstood sieges."

"What say you, Parmenio?" asked a general, turning to King Philip's most trusted adviser.

Parmenio frowned. "If I were Alexander," he answered, "I would bypass Tyre."

Then Alexander spoke, coldly. "If I were Parmenio, I would bypass Tyre. But I am Alexander, and I will take Tyre."

The battle-hardened Parmenio looked at the cocky young king astride Bucephalus. He was reminded of the rash, headstrong boy. "And to take Tyre," he asked, "will your navy appear when you call, or will you bring the mainland to Tyre?"

"Both!" snapped Alexander.

Alexander himself labored alongside his men as they began to build a mole—a raised road into the sea. Made of earth and rock, the mole slowly grew longer and longer until it came within range of the archers and catapults atop Tyre's walls. Arrows and boulders rained down on the invaders.

Alexander's engineers built walls and armed towers on wheels, rolled them to the molehead, and fired back at Tyre.

The Tyrians, in turn, ran fire ships aground on the molehead and burned down the wooden walls and towers.

Months passed. "It's time," said Alexander, "to get my navy."

Cities up and down the coast received his message, "Send me your ships, for I mean to take Tyre." The rulers of these cities knew it was wiser to be Alexander's ally. Alexander got his navy.

Then his engineers contrived a strange fleet of floating siege towers and battering rams. These were mounted on platforms laid across barges. While his fighting ships engaged the Tyrian fleet, Alexander's floating war engines closed in on the doomed city. They battered holes in the walls, and the long seven-month siege ended in a battle of armed men.

Thousands of Tyrians died; thirty thousand survivors were sold into slavery.

Today, after more than two thousand years, Alexander's mole, widened with silt, still connects the island to the mainland.

For the next four years Alexander marched east in triumph. Along the way he founded new cities, all named Alexandria. He led his army over snow-covered mountains and across burning deserts. Many soldiers died. Alexander replaced them with Persians and other Asians, for he had observed how much alike the peoples of different countries were. From being a Greek army it became an international army.

At first Alexander had fought to unite Greece, then to defeat the vast Persian army. Now, having run out of Persians to defeat, Alexander and his unbeaten army continued to make war, seeking ever more power and glory. When he was merciful, Alexander won the loyalty of the conquered nations. But sometimes he was cruel, killing everyone in a defeated city or tribe.

Bucephalus grew weak from age and war wounds. Alexander let his beloved horse rest as much as possible. He rode another horse when marching and when he marshaled his army into battle-ready position. But just before charging into combat, Alexander mounted coal-black Bucephalus. This drew a great cheer from his men, because they believed that if Alexander rode Bucephalus they would be lucky in battle.

Alexander, so restless and curious, was ever seeking: for new lands to conquer; for Ocean, the legendary sea that surrounded all land; for the edge of the world itself. He was unaware that he was one of history's great explorers.

Then a curious thing happened. Alexander and his army marched off the map of the known world. The king and his advisers didn't know where they were. Today we know that they had reached India.

His geographers said, "We are near the top of the world, where Amazons rule. Beware of those mighty women warriors and hunters."

His astronomers said, "Ahead lies Ocean. Beyond its shores giant serpents lurk in dark mists."

"Turn back," warned his seers and priests. "Anger not the gods. Earth's edge is forbidden to man."

But Alexander was Alexander. Astride Bucephalus, he pressed on into India. His soldiers, however, were tired of war. After eight years of marching and fighting they longed to see their homes again. Before them loomed menacing mountains higher than any ever seen. Rumors of Amazon warriors, of serpents and vengeful gods frightened even hardened veterans. "Mad Alexander," they whispered, "founding more Alexandrias."

Still, the army followed where Alexander led. He led them into one of their most difficult battles.

On the far side of a raging rain-swollen river called the Jhelum, a powerful Indian army waited, blocking Alexander's advance. After a dangerous river crossing, his army came up against something new and different: a wall of war elephants.

This strange sight and smell terrified the horses of Alexander's cavalry. Right there on the battlefield Alexander devised a plan to use the Indian elephants against the Indians.

He commanded his archers to pick off the elephant drivers. Then his foot soldiers pressed the Indian soldiers back against the driverless beasts. Meanwhile his archers aimed more arrows at the elephants. Wounded and without their drivers, the towering beasts panicked, trampling their own people as well as Alexander's. The Indian line broke and crumpled in defeat.

During the battle Alexander, as usual, was riding Bucephalus. Suddenly the charger trembled, then fell, lifeless. The strain of the long battle had been too much.

The great Alexander himself led the funeral procession and buried Bucephalus with military honors. On the site Alexander founded another city. For once it was not named Alexandria. This city he named Bucephala.

The rains of India did what no military force could do. It made Alexander and his Grand Army retreat.

The battle of the Jhelum River had ended, but the monsoon downpour went on and on. Everything was soaked. Metal armor and swords rusted, clothing and bedding rotted, food turned moldy, body sores grew, poisonous snakes and clouds of vicious mosquitoes tormented the army. The wet and weary soldiers had no stomach for more wars. The army mutinied, refusing to march on.

Alexander pleaded, promised, threatened, but his men looked at the ground and were silent. In a mad rage the king shut himself in his tent. He refused to speak, eat, see anyone, or change his clothing.

After three days, realizing that his troops would not give in, Alexander chose to save face. He declared craftily, "Let the gods decide!"

His high priests made sacrifices, consulted signs, then wisely divined, "The omens of the gods do not favor a further advance." Thus, accepting the dictate of the gods, Alexander and his army marched back to Persia.

Alexander never returned to his native Greece. He remained in Persia, planning new campaigns.

In 323 B.C., at the age of thirty-three, Alexander died from a disease brought on by exhaustion and old wounds. He had conquered the known world, leaving behind him seventy new cities named Alexandria. More important, he unified the world and showed that people of different races and nations could live and work side by side.

356–323 B.C.